All I Want To Be Is Me

Written and Illustrated by Phyllis Rothblatt, MFT

This is for my children,
who fill my heart with delight.
This is for all children,
in celebration of all of who you are.

I'm the kid with long red hair,
That everybody calls a girl,
But I just like to wear my hair long
'Cuz I love to feel it whirl,
When I'm running with my puppy,
Or climbing in a tree,
I want to be all of me.
All I want to be is me.

I'm the kid with lots of freckles,
I love sports of every kind,
Most people think that I'm a boy,
And I never really mind.
'Cuz ever since I was two I knew
That's who I'm meant to be.
I want to be all of me,
All I want to be is me.

I'm the kid who looks down slowly
When we line up as boys and girls,
I'm not sure which line to go to,
And it makes me want to curl
Into a ball, until you see,
I am so much more than my body.
I want to be all of me,
All I want to be is me.

Don't call me he. Don't call me she.
Please don't assume who I must be.
'Cuz I don't feel like just one of these,
I want to be all of me,
All I want to be is me.

I'm the kid who's great at soccer,
For Christmas I got cleats,
When Grandma tried to get me in a dress,
I told her my new name is Pete.
She looked a little shocked, then a bit surprised,
Then she smiled at me with love in her eyes,
'Cuz she wants me to be all of me,
That's what she wants me to be.

I'm the kid dressed as a princess,
I love really sparkly clothes,
Everybody wonders, but no one really knows
What it's like to be me, in my body.
It takes a lot of courage
To not fit inside a box,
I feel trapped inside a body,
That has so many locks.
But when I look inside my heart,
I am really free.
I want to be all of me,
All I want to be is me.

Don't call me he. Just call me she.
Please don't assume who I must be.
'Cuz I feel like just one of these.
I want to be all of me,
All I want to be is me.

I'm the kid out on the school yard
Other kids like to tease,
They say mean things to hurt me,
And push me to my knees.
But my friends all gather 'round me
And shout out to the bullies,
"We can all be who we want to be!"
"Don't mess with me!"

Don't call me he. Don't call me she.
Please don't assume who I must be.
'Cuz I don't feel like just one of these.
I want to be all of me,
All I want to be is me.

A note for kids ...

There are so many ways to be a boy or a girl and to express who you truly are inside...
Some people may tell you, "That's a boy thing!" or "You can't do that- that's just for
girls!" But no one else can tell you who you really are inside, or what's okay to like!

What really matters, is that you like yourself for who you are. The world would be a
boring place if everyone were the same. What makes this a beautiful, colorful
world is each one of us getting to be all of whom we are.

I hope that you feel celebrated and know that just by being you, you add to the
beauty of the world!

Follow your heart!
Love, Phyllis

On this page, draw a picture of yourself- just being you and doing what you love.
You can also write your own verse about who you are.
(If you want, you can send me your picture, and I'll add it to my website!)

About the author:

Phyllis Rothblatt is an artist, writer, educator, and licensed marriage and family therapist in the SF Bay Area. For over twenty years, she has worked with families of all kinds, including families with gender non-conforming and transgender children and youth. She teaches and offers trainings for parents, professionals and community groups around the country, on issues facing gender variant children and their families. She also offers expressive arts workshops for children, youth and families. She is passionate about creating a conscious community of support for all families that celebrates the unique gifts of every child.

To order more books, or to download the original version of the song, "*All I Want To Be Is Me*", please visit her website at www.alliwanttobeisme.com. For more information about her workshops, training, consultation or therapy services, please contact Phyllis at phyllis.rothblatt@gmail.com.